©2020 CHOUETTE PUBLISHING (1987) INC.
Original title: Alya et les trois chats
Text: Amina Hachimi Alaoui
Illustrations: Maya Fidawi
©2016 Yankow Al Kitab

CrackBoom! Books is an imprint of Chouette Publishing (1987) Inc.

Translation: Nathaniel Penn

Chouette Publishing would like to thank the Government of Canada and SODEC for their financial support.

Canada Québec
Books
Tax Credit Gestion
SODEC

Bibliothèque et Archives nationales du Québec and Library and Archives Canada cataloguing in publication

Title: Alya and the three cats / text, Amina Hachimi Alaoui; illustrations, Maya Fidawi; translation, Mehdi Retnani.

Other titles: 'Alyā' wa al-qiṭaṭ al-talāt. English

Names: Hachimi Alaoui, Amina, author. | Fidawi, Maya, illustrator. | Retnani, Mehdi, translator.

Description: Translation of: Alya et les trois chats, which is the translation of: 'Alyā' wa al-qiṭaṭ al-talāt.

Identifiers: Canadiana 20190035196 | ISBN 9782898022364 (hardcover)

Classification: LCC PZ7.1.H33 Al 2020 | DDC j892.73/7—dc23

Legal deposit – Bibliothèque et Archives nationales du Québec, 2020.
Legal deposit – Library and Archives Canada, 2020.

CRACKBOOM! BOOKS

©2020 Chouette Publishing (1987) Inc.
1001 Lenoir St., Suite B-238
Montreal, Quebec H4C 2Z6 Canada
crackboombooks.com

Printed in China
10 9 8 7 6 5 4 3 2 1 CHO2091 DEC2019

Alya

and the
Three
Cats

Text: Amina Hachimi Alaoui
Illustrations: Maya Fidawi
Translation: Nathaniel Penn

CRACKBOOM!

Minouche, Pasha, and Amir live peacefully
in Myriam and Sami's home.
They are treated like princes, and they spend
their time lounging around and playing.
They purr when Myriam strokes them.

Pasha has long black fur
and green eyes.
Exquisite and regal, he stares
intensely at the others.
He looks like a real pasha!

Minouche's gray coat is striped like a tiger's.
Solitary and shy, she likes to find places to hide.
Is it possible she remembers the cold and rainy day
when Myriam found her in the street?

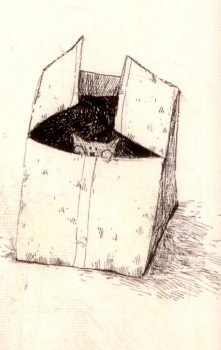

Amir, the Siamese, is curious
and always in motion.
He loves to play with his ball;
he takes small swipes at it with
his paws. He follows Myriam
everywhere, and sometimes
even gets tangled up in her feet.

The three cats love to curl up
on Myriam's belly.
But Myriam's belly is growing
every day... The cats' favorite place
to snuggle get higher and higher.

One day, the cats actually see Myriam's belly move.
Only Amir is brave enough to go closer. He listens
carefully: Thump-thump, thump-thump.
What could be inside?
Pasha looks at the huge belly in astonishment.
Minouche backs away... and sits on the edge
of the bed.

Early one morning, Myriam and Sami leave home
suddenly.
Where can they be going at this early hour,
without so much as a good-morning caress—
without even saying goodbye?

With Myriam gone, the nights and days are long.
The cats wait in front of the closed door for her return.
Finally she comes home again, with a pretty basket in her arms.

Myriam enters the bedroom
without even looking at the cats.
What's going on?
Where did her big belly go?
What's inside the basket she's carrying?

Sami pushes the bedroom door open...
The cats glimpse a funny little creature in the basket.
It wriggles! It squeaks like a mouse!

Noticing how curious they are, Grandma
reassures them:

"My sweet cats, say hello to Alya. She was
just born.

From now on, Myriam will take care of you
and the baby too. To love is to share. "

The cats look at each other anxiously.
"Share? How?" There are three of us already!
They start meowing and dashing around
the room nervously.

As Alya sleeps peacefully in her baby carriage, Myriam bends down to pet the three cats. "There is enough love in my heart for Alya and for you," she whispers to them. "Don't worry!"

Now the cats are calm and confident again.
Pasha stands guard beside the baby carriage.
Amir helps Grandma open all the presents. Playing with the ribbons is his favorite game.
Minouche watches the door so no one can disturb their new life.

A life full of love and tenderness.